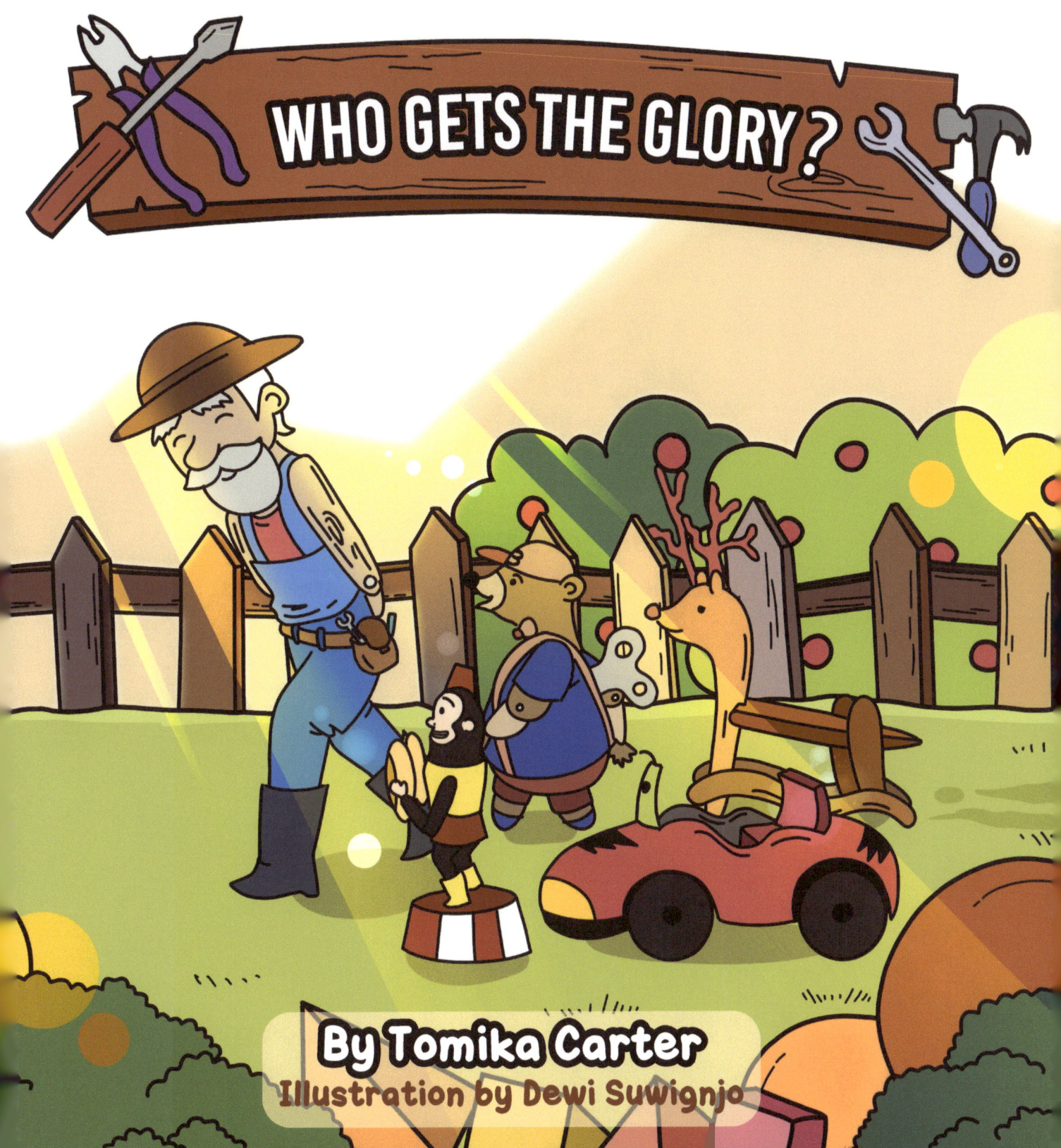

WHO GETS THE GLORY ?

By Tomika Carter

Illustration by Dewi Suwignjo

This book is dedicated to everyone who reads it.
It is a friendly reminder of God's greatness.

²³Thus says the L ord:

"Let not the wise man glory in his wisdom,
Let not the mighty man glory in his might,
Nor let the rich man glory in his riches;
²⁴But let him who glories glory in this,
That he understands and knows Me,
That I am the L ord, exercising lovingkindness,
judgment, and righteousness in the earth.
For in these I delight," says the L ord.

Jeremiah 9:23–24 NKJV

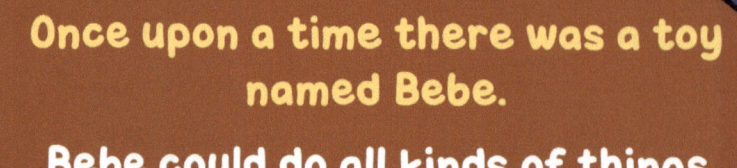

Once upon a time there was a toy named Bebe.

Bebe could do all kinds of things like sing, dance and read stories at bedtime.

He bragged to all his other toy friends about all the things he could do.

Some of the other toys used to be very fun to play with but they had buttons missing and some no longer worked at all.

One day he was singing a song and noticed the notes were not on key.

His battery was dying, and he soon realized that his power was coming from a source other than himself.

He went to his manual and found out who the toy maker was and planned a visit.

TOY MAKER

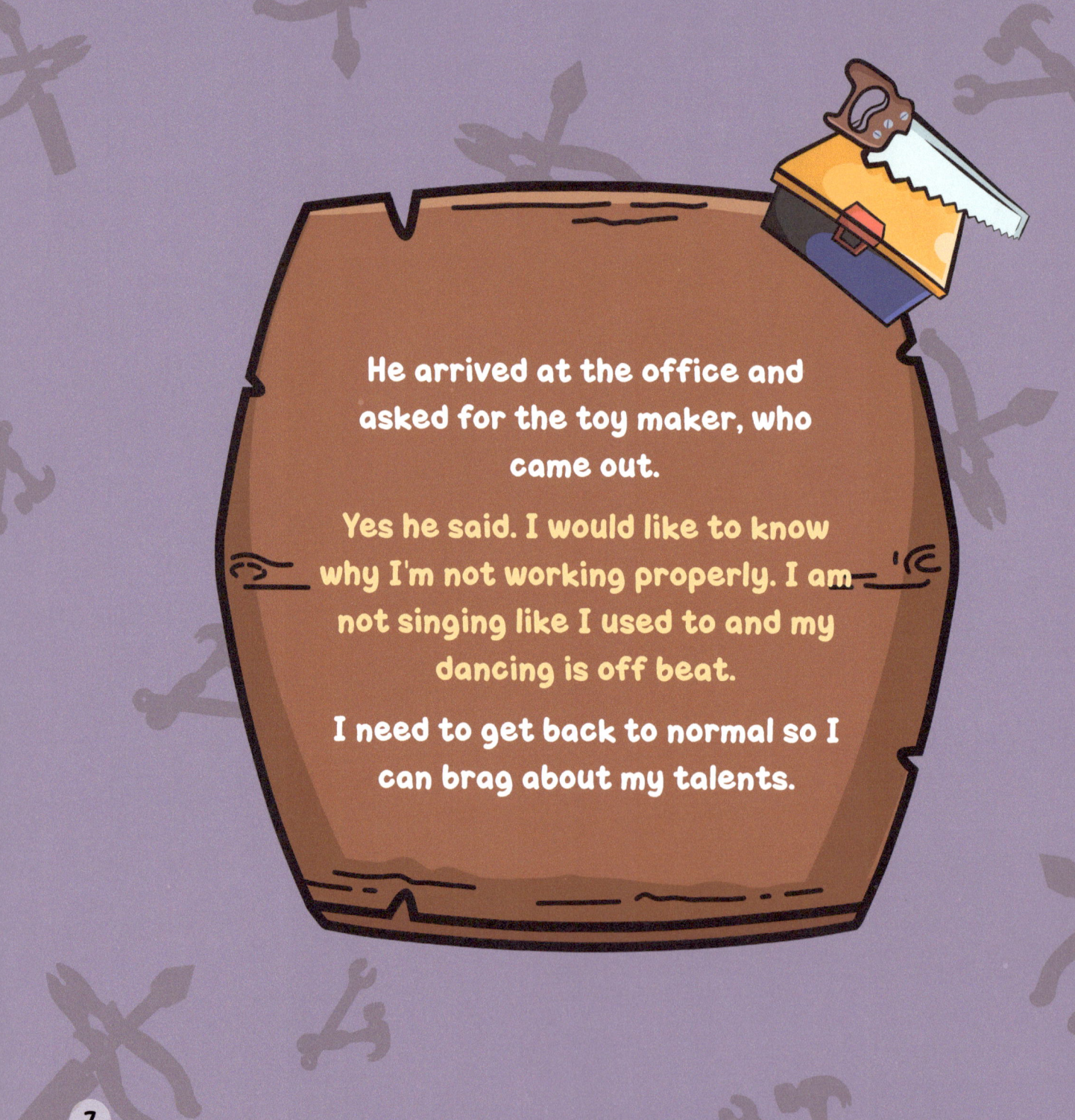

He arrived at the office and asked for the toy maker, who came out.

Yes he said. I would like to know why I'm not working properly. I am not singing like I used to and my dancing is off beat.

I need to get back to normal so I can brag about my talents.

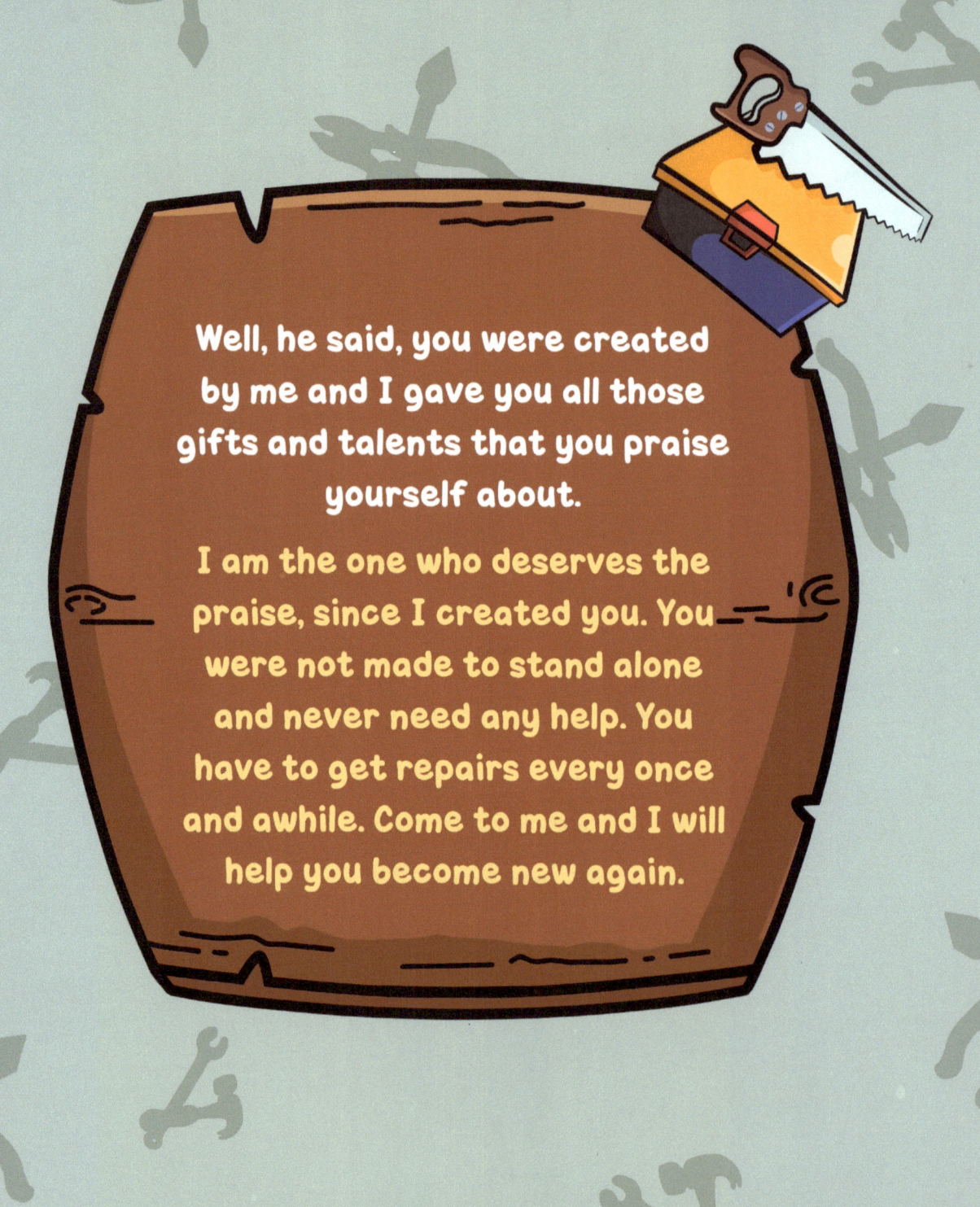

Well, he said, you were created by me and I gave you all those gifts and talents that you praise yourself about.

I am the one who deserves the praise, since I created you. You were not made to stand alone and never need any help. You have to get repairs every once and awhile. Come to me and I will help you become new again.

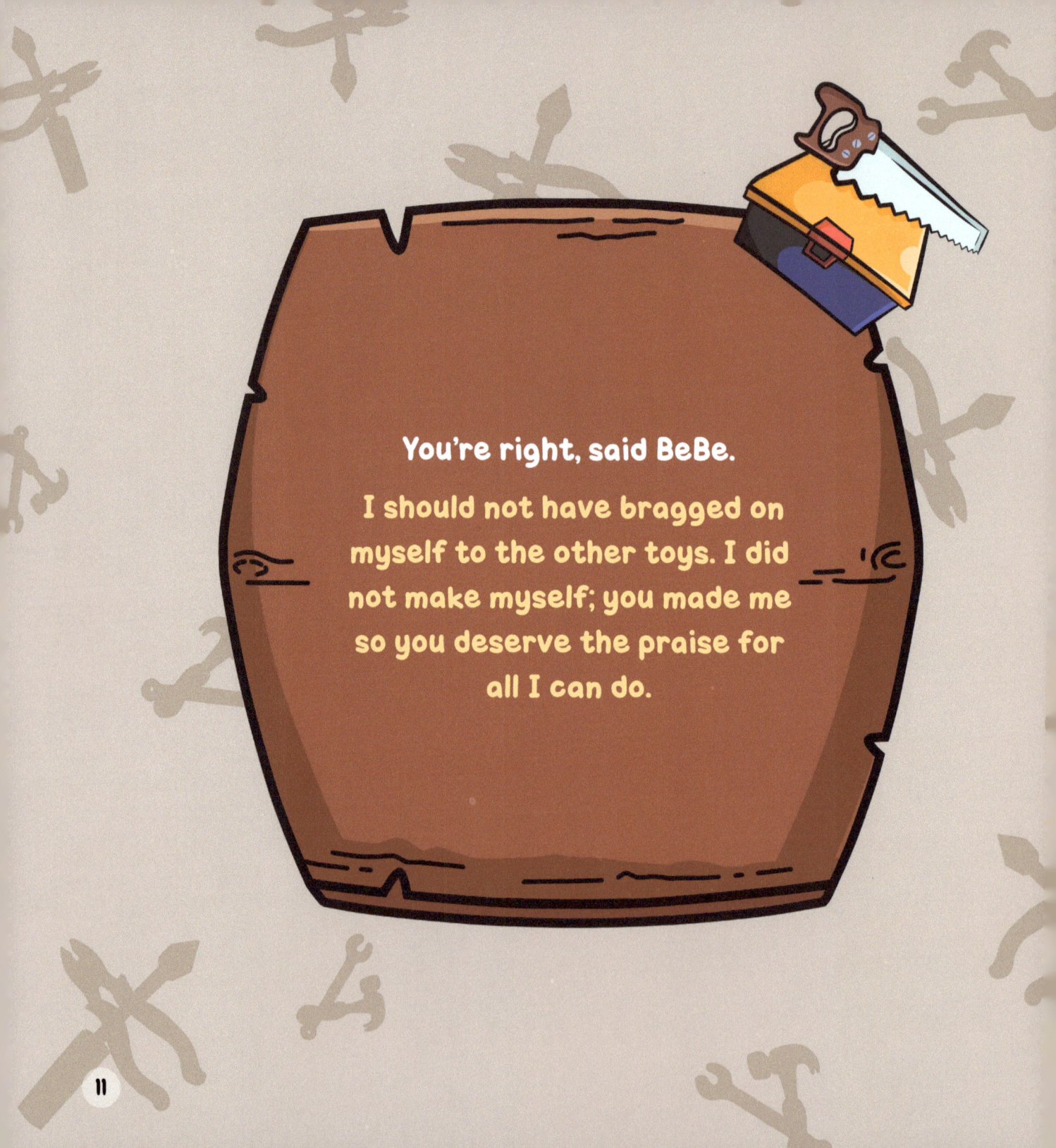

You're right, said BeBe.

I should not have bragged on myself to the other toys. I did not make myself; you made me so you deserve the praise for all I can do.

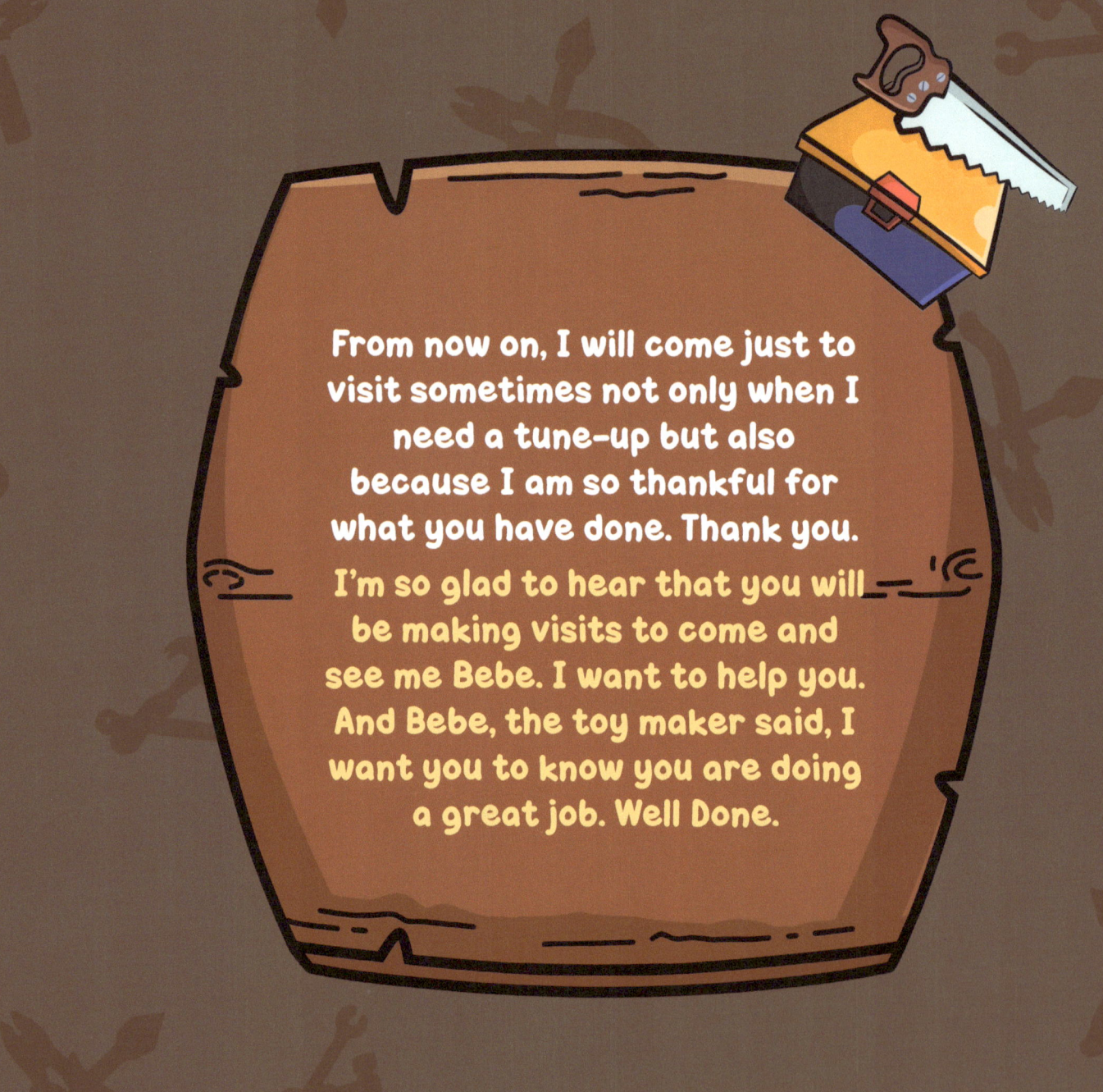

From now on, I will come just to visit sometimes not only when I need a tune-up but also because I am so thankful for what you have done. Thank you.

I'm so glad to hear that you will be making visits to come and see me Bebe. I want to help you. And Bebe, the toy maker said, I want you to know you are doing a great job. Well Done.

I sure am, I mean Thank You.

Bebe went back to his home and told all the other toys what had happened and all about the toy maker.

They were amazed at all he learned. They also wanted to meet the toy maker so that they could be put back together again and show their gratitude.

From that day forward Bebe no longer bragged on himself but gave all the glory to the one who made him — Toy Maker, also known as

The Creator.

THE END

About the author

Tomika Arnold-Carter is an author and owner of Robert Thomas Publishing. Tomika's books include the children's book and song "I'm Ok" and finance book "Apples 2 Apples". For more information about Tomika, visit her website www.queensentertainment.com, follow her on Instagram @robertthomaspublishing or Like her Facebook fan page at www.facebook.com/robertthomaspublishing